Mia's
Quiet
Day

by Anne Sibley O'Brien

illustrated by Rebecca Allen James

Macmillan
McGraw-Hill

New York   Farmington

Mia frowned at the rain.

She was stuck inside.

She picked up her donkey.

"Remember, Sam," she said.

"We have to be quiet.

Mom has lots of work to do before lunch."

Mia looked at her desk.

Scissors were quiet.

She folded a sheet of paper.

She began to cut.

Snip, snip, snip.

It was Sam!

"Hee-haw!" Mia whispered.

The dancing lady hit her toe
on a book.

Books were quiet.

The book was about a pirate.

Mia stood on her ship.

"Yo-ho-ho!" she whispered.

She searched the seas
for treasure.

And there it was!

Her paint box was full of color,
like jewels.

Paints were quiet.

Mia forgot the rainstorm.

She painted and painted.

Then she heard a loud noise.

"BEEP-BEEP-BEEP!"

"Oh! Oh, no!"

The noise was coming from her mom's room.

Mia went to see.

"Shhh!

Quiet in here!" Mia said.

"My mom's trying to work!"

Mom started to laugh, and so did Mia.

And they laughed just as loud
as they wanted.